THIS BOOK BELONGS TO:

_____

_____

Free Bonus Gift Giveaway!!

Sign up on explorearthursworld.com to receive your gift!

ISBN: 978-1-950904-16-7 (eBook)
ISBN: 978-1-950904-17-4 (Paperback)
ISBN: 978-1-950904-18-1 (Hardcover)
Library of Congress Control Number: TXu002184827
Edited by Jennifer Rees
Cover design and Illustrations by Judith San Nicolás (JudithSDesign&Creativity)

ARTHUR GOES BACK TO SCHOOL

GENE LIPEN

With school supplies packed, and his clothes nice and clean,
Arthur is ready to learn, play, and win.
Let's wish him the best on his journey and state:
"A Back-to-School venture,
We just cannot wait!"

We get so excited and stand with no fuss,
The first time we wait for a ride on the bus.
When the door opens up, we're welcomed aboard,
By a smiling driver who is watching the road.
We pick out our seat and enjoy the quick ride,
While exchanging our stories with new friends inside.

SCHOOL BUS

Excitement becomes very hard to contain,
When we spot our school building, down a beautiful lane.
It is time to jump off and we are ready to dart,
A learning adventure, is about to start.

If conquering numbers is the goal that you seek,
The subject of Math performs this magic trick.
It will reward you with knowledge that is simple to use,
In our daily lives, so make sure not to snooze.
Addition and Subtraction can be hard to explain,

$$5 - 4 = 1$$

$$2 + 1 = 3$$

Math

But, what seems like a challenge,
you will learn to make plain.
When a problem is raised, it is your time to shine,
And share with others how the answers align.
Stay focused and sharp with so much to amass,
And you'll feel a little smarter, every time you leave class.

Without this class, you won't get very far,
It will teach you to read and to write like a star.
At first, learning letters and multiple sounds,
Might seem harder than lifting one thousand pounds!
Yet, once you get started, you will quickly uncover,
Fun and simple rules to apply and discover.

You will feel like you are putting together a puzzle,
While slowly improving your brain's reading muscle.
With so many books in the world to explore,
Once you begin reading, life won't be a bore.

Ready to take a quick break from your studies,
And enjoy some free time outside with school buddies?
Let imagination be your trusty guide,
As you think of the games that you can't play inside.
From hopscotch and slides, to good old hide and seek,
There is so much to do, so try something unique!

Discover new friends and have lots of fun,
While enjoying fresh air and the wonderful sun.
The problem with Recess: it's as quick as a puff—
No matter how long, it is never enough.

recess

Constantly changing, but always in style,
The power of Music has been around a long while.
It can lift you to highs when you are feeling down,
And leave you with a smile, instead of a frown.
In this class you'll learn how the music we make,
Can be written on paper, without any mistake.

Playing different instruments is lots of fun—
You should certainly try to enjoy every one.
Uncover your secret potential in time,
As you practice daily and help your skills climb.

Have you ever wondered what makes flowers grow,
Or could not figure out how water can flow?
These types of questions Science tries to address—
Our world is full of puzzles, but there is no need to stress.

You will learn how to think in a different way,
Using logic to explain what we see every day.
Life is full of amazement, so it's not a surprise,
That we miss Science daily, right in front of our eyes.
Questions always evolve and don't stand in one place,
But the answers we find, help the entire human race.

If running and jumping is your cup of tea,
Then the class of Phys Ed, is the right place to be.
Put on your sports clothes and sneakers to match,
And get super excited to run, jump, and catch.
There are so many games that are easy to play—

Each one fun and unique in a different way.
Regular exercise will keep you strong and fit,
So do your very best and make sure not to quit.
With so many options to choose every day,
You will get many chances to put your skills on display.

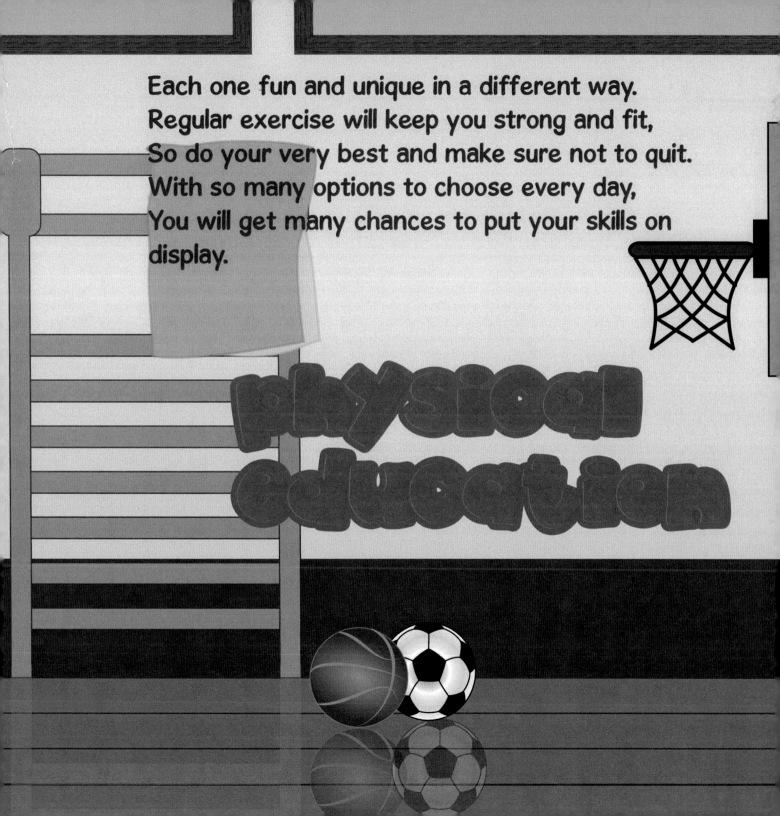

With countless people and timeless traditions,
This class takes us daily into traveling missions.
So many countries call our planet home—
Some with famous, old cities, like Athens and Rome.

geography

All of them different in their own special way,
You'll learn something amazing and new every day.
Discover new cultures and what makes them unique,
From different clothes, to the language they speak.
Explore faraway lands, oceans, rivers and seas,
All your questions, in time, will be answered with ease!

With so many activities to try after school,
You are sure to find something amazing and cool.
From sports that will help you get better and train,
To science and math clubs that challenge your brain.

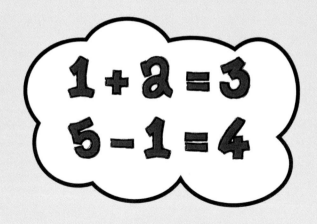

Theater will give you a chance to express,
The artist inside and the talent you possess.
No matter what interesting path you will take,
Your parents will be proud of decisions you make.
It is hard to go wrong with whatever you choose—
Try them all if you can, there is nothing to lose.

Getting home is exciting—we don't want to delay,
Sharing all the great stories that touched us today.
We enjoy family dinner every night of the week,
Even if we get interrupted when trying to speak.

coming home

It is time for our homework, important and wise,
Since it helps take the lessons we learned to new highs.
And when late in the evening our bedtime arrives,
We think of tomorrow, while rubbing our eyes.
A sweet, gentle smile comes over our face,
As dreams take us away to a magical place.

Thank you for reading our Back-to-School book,
It was a fun, educational ride that we took.
This story is ending, but we all can assume,
Another Arthur adventure will be coming soon!

Thank you for reading. If you enjoyed this book, please consider leaving an honest review at your favorite store.

Check out more books about Arthur in the Kids Books For Young Explorers series

I LIKE THIS BOOK, BECAUSE:

_____

_____

Made in the USA
Las Vegas, NV
10 December 2020